The Easter story, based on readings from the four gospels, retold using simple language for young listeners and early readers.

British Library Cataloguing in Publication Data
Hately, David
    The Easter story.
    1. Easter
    I. Title   II. Geary, Robert   III. Series
    394.2'68283
    ISBN 0-7214-9611-3

First edition

Published by Ladybird Books Ltd Loughborough Leicestershire UK
Ladybird Books Inc Auburn Maine 04210 USA
© LADYBIRD BOOKS LTD MCMXC
Printed in England

FIRST BIBLE STORIES

The Easter Story

by DAVID HATELY

illustrated by ROBERT GEARY

Ladybird Books

Jesus was a great and good teacher. He lived in Galilee and walked from village to village, healing the sick and telling people about the Kingdom of God.

He taught that the best way to love God is to love and care for other people.

Jesus chose twelve disciples to help him in his work.

Three times he told them that he would be killed by enemies who hated him. But he also said that on the third day after his death, he would rise again.

The disciples did not know what Jesus meant. How could a dead man come back to life?

When Jesus decided that his work in Galilee was finished, he took his disciples to the city of Jerusalem.

He rode into the city on a donkey. The people spread their cloaks out like a carpet to welcome him. Everyone waved palm branches and shouted *Hosanna!* as he passed by.

When Jesus visited the Temple in Jerusalem, he found it full of merchants, buying and selling as if they were in a marketplace.

Jesus was so angry that he drove the merchants out of the Temple and knocked their stalls to the ground.

'My house is a house of prayer,' he
shouted, 'but you have made it a den of
thieves!'

Many important people in Jerusalem hated Jesus. They said he had no right to teach in the Temple. They were jealous, too, because everyone loved Jesus.

Jesus' enemies wanted to kill him, but were afraid to seize him during the day when the crowds were listening to him.

Every night, Jesus slept in the open air on a hill called the Mount of Olives. Only his friends knew this.

One evening, the disciple called Judas Iscariot slipped away to see the enemies of Jesus.

'Give me some money,' said Judas, 'and I will tell you where Jesus is. Then you can capture him secretly, without anyone knowing.'

The enemies of Jesus gave Judas thirty silver coins and set out for the Mount of. Olives carrying clubs and swords.

'How will we know which one is Jesus?' they asked Judas.

'Leave it to me,' he answered.

When they arrived, Judas went up to Jesus and kissed him. 'Master,' he whispered.

So the enemies of Jesus knew that this was the man they were looking for.

Jesus was treated like a criminal. He was put on trial and sentenced to death.

Soldiers forced him to carry a heavy wooden cross to a hill called Calvary. Then they nailed him to the cross and left him to die.

To make sure that he was dead, one of the soldiers drove a spear into Jesus' side.

When Jesus was dead and the soldiers had gone, the disciples and other friends took Jesus' body down from the cross.

They wrapped it in linen and placed it in a
tomb cut from rock. Then they rolled a
heavy stone in front of the tomb to close it.

On the morning of the third day after Jesus' death, some women went to visit the tomb.

To their astonishment, the heavy stone had been rolled back from the tomb. As they stood there, wondering what had happened, two angels in brilliant clothes appeared at their side.

'Jesus is not here,' they said. 'He has risen from the dead! Remember what he said in Galilee!'

The women ran to tell the disciples, but at first no one believed them.

Then, during the days that followed, Jesus himself came to talk to some of his friends.

But one disciple, called Thomas, was never present. He refused to believe that Jesus was alive unless he could actually touch Jesus' scars.

Eight days later, Jesus came to see the disciples again.

'Peace!' he said. Then he showed Thomas the scars in his hands and side. 'Touch them!' said Jesus.

But Thomas fell to his knees. 'You are my Lord and God!' he answered.

'You believe because you can see me,' Jesus said, 'but happy are those who believe even though they cannot see me!'

Jesus did not stay long with his friends. He told them that he was returning to heaven to be with his Father.

After he had left them, the disciples travelled to many countries and told the people about Jesus and his teachings.

Those who follow the teachings of Jesus are called Christians. They believe that Jesus is the son of God. At Christmas they celebrate his birth. On Good Friday they mourn his death. And at Easter they are happy because they remember that he rose in triumph from the dead.